Introduction

Most parents are uncomfortable talking about poop. They are also uncomfortable when their children talk about poop. Unfortunately, when families do not talk about poop, children are more likely to become constipated.

Most of the time pooping is easy but when occasional constipation occurs it stops being easy. If a parent is unaware that their child is constipated or does not manage it properly, occasional constipation can quickly become a more serious condition known as functional constipation or encopresis. Functional constipation can last for a year or longer and can cause children to withhold stool and accidentally poop in their underwear. Currently, more than four million children in the United States have functional constipation.

It is my hope that this book will help prevent severe childhood constipation by educating children and parents and by facilitating healthy parent-child conversations about poop.

Thomas R. DuHamel, PhD

Copyright © 2015 by Thomas R. DuHamel

Maret Publishing
P.O. Box 25606
Seattle, Washington 98165

Illustrations, Cover Design and Layout:
Kev Brockschmidt

ISBN: 978-0-9854969-3-7
Library of Congress Control Number: 2014915182

Printed in the United States of America
First Edition
First Printing

SOFTY THE POOP
Helping Families Talk About Poop

Written by
Thomas R. DuHamel, PhD

Illustrated by
Kev Brockschmidt

Maret Publishing

Meet Softy the Poop.

Softty likes to be soft like toothpaste,

long and smooth

like a banana

or a snake

and light brown
or green like a
frog.

But, sometimes, Softy gets

hard like
a rock,

lumpy like a
baby camel,

round like a ball

and dark
brown like
a chocolate
fudge brownie.

Kids hold Softy inside too long

and
sometimes
it hurts
when a
hard Softy
comes
out.

What Softy really, really likes is to dive into its swimming pool,

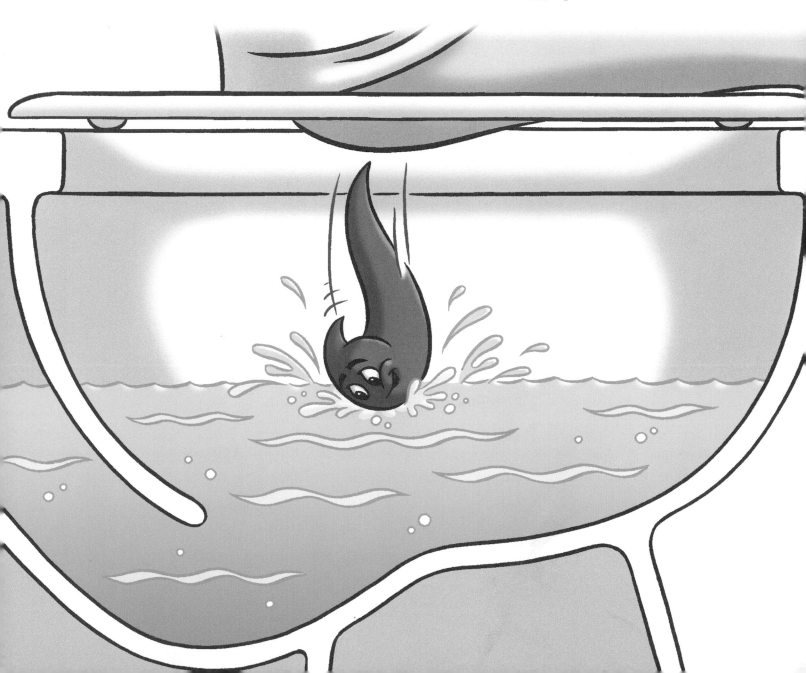

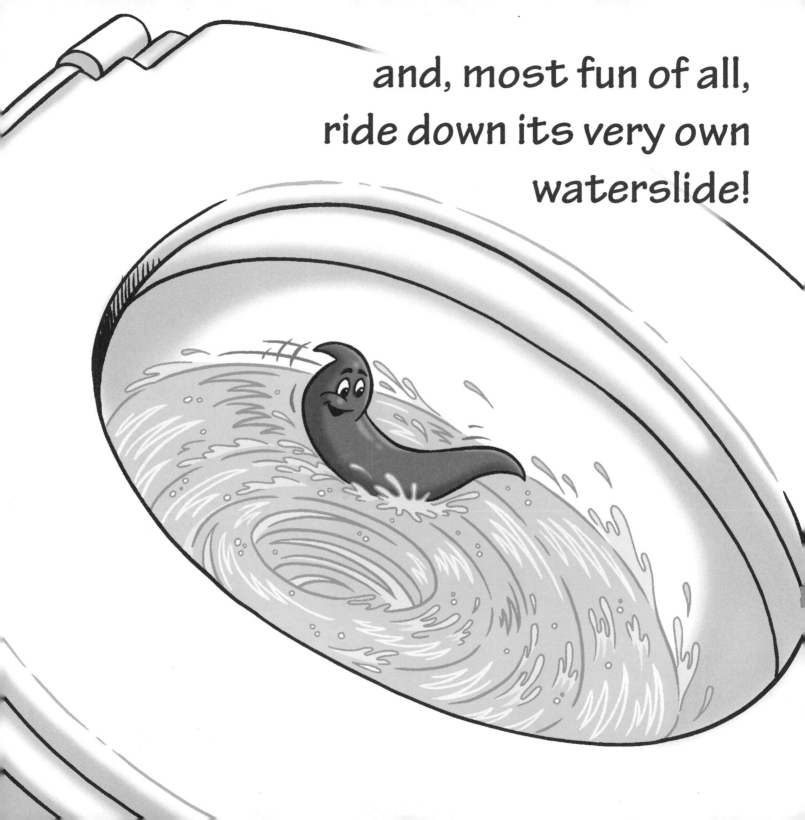

and, most fun of all,
ride down its very own
waterslide!

Please help Softy the Poop stay soft. Eat Softy's favorite foods like

green peas,

 raspberries

and popcorn.

Drink Softy's favorite drinks like

water   and milk

and push Softy
out to play
every day.

Before you flush Softy down its waterslide, don't forget to call mommy and daddy,

don't forget to wipe your bottom

and don't forget to say, "Bye, Bye Softy. I'll see you again tomorrow."

Poop Notes for Parents

Meet Softy the Poop.
Normal stool is shaped like a snake or a banana with tapered ends. It has a smooth surface, a consistency similar to that of toothpaste and comes in all shades of brown and green.

But, sometimes, Softy gets constipated.
Constipated stool is much dryer and denser than normal stool. It is often round, ranging in size from a rabbit pellet to a tennis ball or it may look like a sausage with lumps and cracks on the surface. The color of constipated stool ranges from dark brown to almost black. Black stool should be brought to the attention of your healthcare provider.

This makes Softy the Poop very sad because it can hurt.
Dry stool is difficult to pass and it sometimes hurts when it comes out. After one or more uncomfortable or painful bowel movements, some children begin to hold back or withhold their stool in order to avoid more discomfort or pain. Continued withholding can lead to severe childhood constipation.

What Softy really, really likes is to come out to play every day.
Children will often ignore the urge to defecate because they do not want to stop playing or because sitting on the toilet is boring. Thinking about Softy the Poop will make bowel movements more enjoyable, almost like meeting a friend every day.

Continues on next page

Please help Softy the Poop stay soft.
Stool softness is related to the consumption of fiber and liquids and to the frequency of bowel movements. The amount of fiber recommended for toddlers and preschoolers is the age of the child plus 5 grams. For example, a 3-year old child should consume a minimum of 8 grams of fiber daily which is equivalent to 1 cup of raspberries or 1 cup of cooked green peas or 8 cups of air-popped white popcorn.

Children in this age group should drink a minimum of 4 to 5 cups of liquid a day. Cow's milk is sometimes constipating but not always. Unless a child has a known allergy to cow's milk or eats large amounts of dairy products, milk is unlikely to cause constipation. When in doubt, try a milk substitute.

There is no "normal" when it comes to the frequency of bowel movements. Every child has his or her own schedule. However, a noticeable decrease in the usual frequency of a child's bowel movements or fewer than three bowel movements a week may be signs of constipation.

Look at your child's stool.
The incidence of severe childhood constipation is highest in children 1 to 6 years of age. This is partly due to the fact that parents rarely look at their child's stool and therefore do not know if their child's bowel movements are normal or constipated. In order to avoid severe childhood constipation, parents should look at their child's stool at least every 2 or 3 days.

About the author

Thomas R. DuHamel, PhD is a pediatric psychologist and clinical associate professor in the Department of Psychiatry and Behavioral Sciences at the University of Washington School of Medicine. Dr. DuHamel specializes in the prevention and treatment of childhood constipation and is author of "The Ins and Outs of Poop: A Guide to Treating Childhood Constipation," a book for parents and healthcare providers.

Dr. Tom answers questions and offers telephone consultations at www.TheInsandOutsofPoop.com.

About the illustrator

Kevin "KEV" Brockschmidt is a freelance cartoon illustrator living near Seattle, Washington. Most of his work is for children including games, books, magazines, internet and educational materials. He recently illustrated three books in the "Pocketdoodles" series from Gibbs Smith - "City Doodles San Francisco," "Cowboy Doodles" and "Texas Doodles."

Visit www.kevscartoons.com to see samples of his artwork.

Pictures of poop drawn by kids like you.

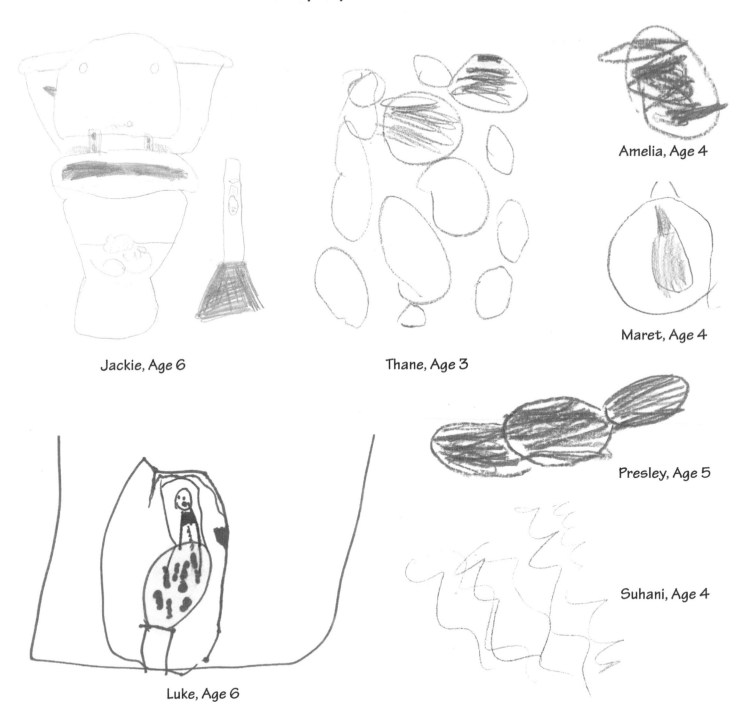

Jackie, Age 6

Thane, Age 3

Amelia, Age 4

Maret, Age 4

Presley, Age 5

Luke, Age 6

Suhani, Age 4

Draw your own picture of poop.

Draw your own picture of poop.

Dr. Tom's companion book for parents and healthcare providers is available at

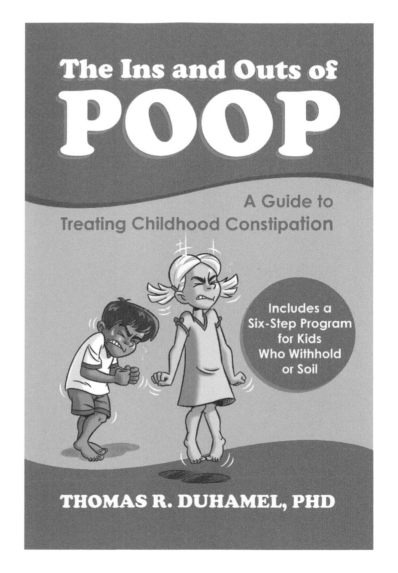

To learn more about childhood constipation, visit:

www.TheInsandOutsofPoop.com

CPSIA information can be obtained at www.ICGtesting.com
Printed in the USA
LVOW01s2324181114

414428LV00015B/38/P